ABBY
TRAVELS TO
SOUTH AFRICA

BY
LINKY UGEH

ILLUSTRATED BY
B. HUZAIFAH

DEDICATION

This book is dedicated to my munchkins:
Rorisang, Remoratile, Noah and Nathaniel.

Thank you for making traveling interesting and
encouraging me to view the world with new eyes.

Remember to soak in the beauty, smile for the camera,
send a postcard home... and always
say yes to an adventure.

"Do you have your passport?" her dad asked.
"Yes," she said, as she waved it in front of him.

They checked their luggage in at the counter and headed to the boarding gate. The airport was bigger than she expected. There were people everywhere and people calling different destinations on the loud speaker.

Boarding

She slept and woke up and they still weren't there yet, so she watched a movie to keep her busy.

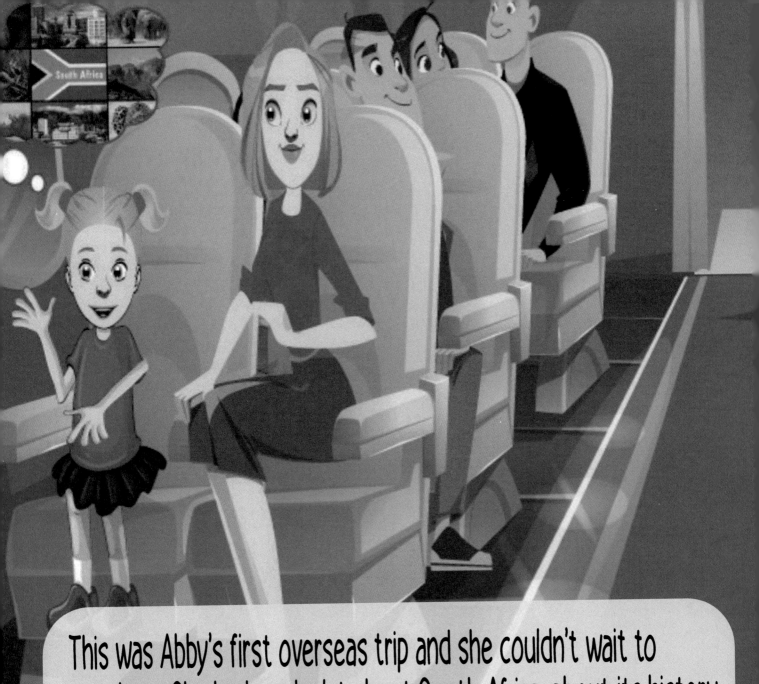

This was Abby's first overseas trip and she couldn't wait to get there. She had read a lot about South Africa, about its history, its people and all the places they would visit.

"Sanibonani (Sun-boh-nah-nee) and welcome to South Africa," the flight attendant said as they finally landed. She had read that Sanibonani means hello in isiZulu which is one of South Africa's 11 official languages they spoke in South Africa.

They arrived at the hotel in Cape Town and were greeted by music from a marimba band. Marimba is an African instrument similar to a xylophone. She couldn't wait for the start of their tour the next day.

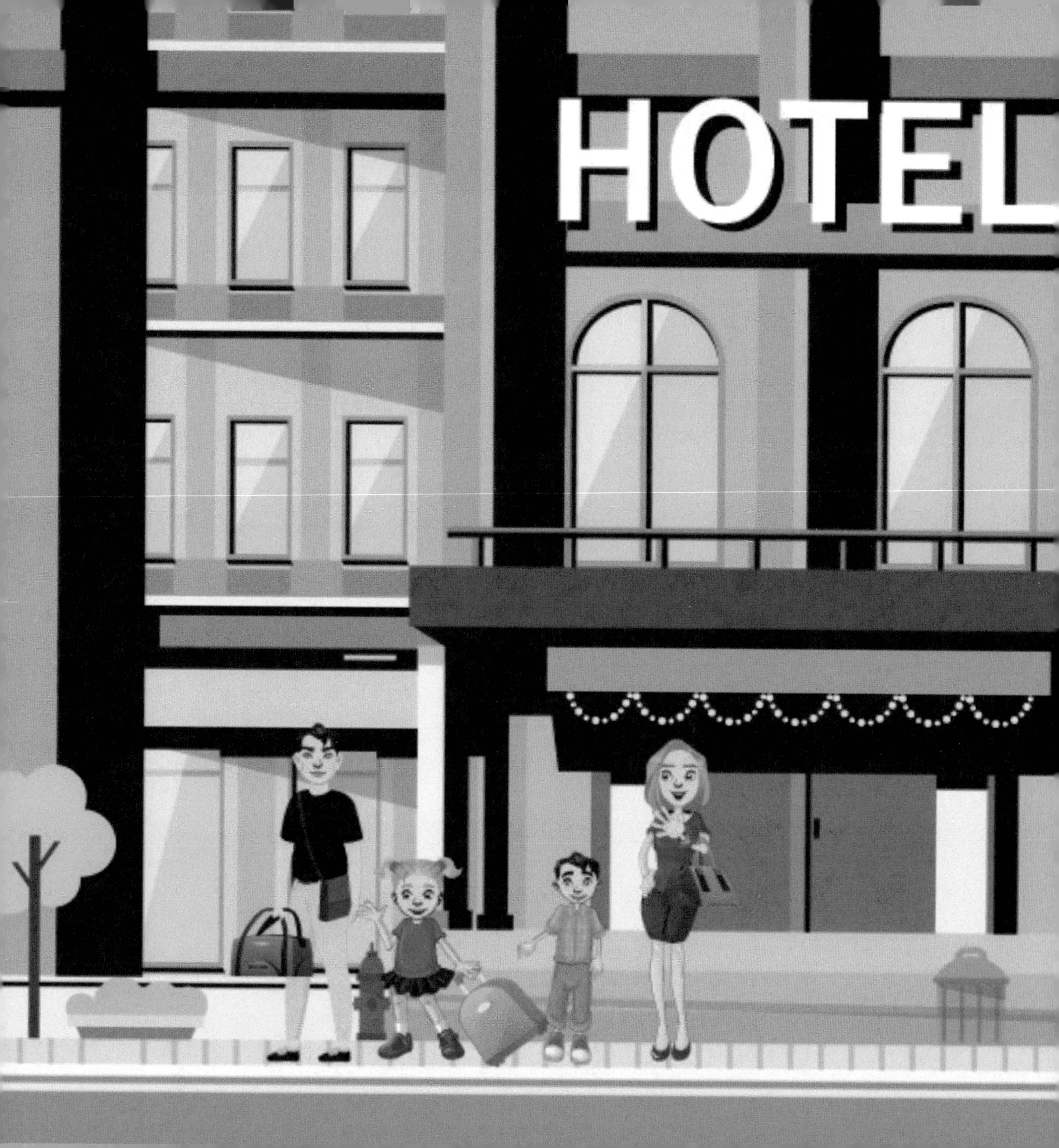
HOTEL

The Western Cape, where Cape Town is, is famous for Table Mountain. It is also famous for the place where the Atlantic Ocean and the Indian Ocean meet, and for being the southern-most tip of Africa.

Their first stop was the famous Table Mountain where they took a cable car to get to the top.

Table Mountain is one of the New 7 Wonders of Nature and has been around for over six million years. She could see the whole city from the top.

They drove around the city tasting all the different food like koeksisters (kook-sis-terrs) which are a baked treat covered in syrup.

They obviously couldn't leave without visiting the beach. Her brother liked that the most. While playing, she made a new friend, Naledi, who was also on holiday. Naledi explained that her name means star in Setswana, another one of South Africa's languages.

The Kruger National Park is one of the oldest and largest game reserves in Africa. She had read about the animals known as the Big 5 and had her camera ready to show her friends back home.

The Big 5 includes the lion, leopard, black rhino, buffalo and elephant. The Big 5 is famous because when hunters used to hunt on foot these animals were the most dangerous to hunt.

Abby was enjoying her trip so much she didn't realize it was close to ending. She had one more place to visit before going back to Omaha, Nebraska.

After a long drive, they arrived in Johannesburg, also known as the City of Gold. This big city was very similar to hers with its tall buildings.

Abby was amazed when they walked down Vilakazi (vee-lah-kah-zee) street in Soweto (So-weh-toe). Soweto is a township in Johannesburg. There were people wearing traditional African prints, with stalls selling all sorts of African arts and crafts. There were beads, dolls and clothes.

The tour guide took them to see Nelson Mandela's house and told them about apartheid (ah-paar-tate), which was a time when there was segregation amongst races.

She was also able to taste more of the traditional foods at the end of their tour. she couldn't remember all the names but she did remember pap (puh-p) which had a sticky texture and was made from mealie meal, and boerewors (boor-uh-vors) which is a sausage unique to South Africa.

There were so many other places she wished they could have visited like Durban and the Cradle of Humankind but there just wasn't enough time.

She had watched a video about the fossils, tools and traces of early humans that were as old as 3 million years or more, which could be seen at the Cradle of Humankind's Maropeng (Mah-ruh-peng) visitor center. She would have to go there next time.

It was going to be a long flight back so Abby went to bed early that night.

She couldn't wait to show her friends all the pictures she had taken and tell them about all the places she had been to.

On the plane Abby sat with her new Ndebele (Nn-deh-beh-leh) cultural doll next to her. These were special handmade dolls which are known for their beautiful, detailed beadwork.

She gazed out of the window saying one final goodbye to the beautiful country she had just visited. She had had a wonderful trip to South Africa that she would never forget.

AUTHOR BIO

As an author and advocate for women's empowerment,
Linky believes that the way we experience life, is the way we tell it.
Having had the opportunity to travel around the world as a child
to countries such as Egypt, France, Malaysia, Singapore and others,
she found that those experiences influenced her view of the world
and exposed her to people, places and tastes she would otherwise
not have encountered.

Linky's work in women's empowerment started at the
Graça Machel Trust based in South Africa, and has continued as
the Communications Coordinator of Purposeful Living INC, an Indiana
based women's nonprofit.

Her 4 exuberant children inspired her to write a children's travel
series, starting with her home country of South Africa. She dreams
of lounging on the beach with her husband, no kids in tow, to enjoy
the sights depicted in her books. Abby Travels is the first in the series.

COMING SOON

In the next book, join Tanisha as she travels from New York to West Africa with her mom.

Can you guess which country she visits?
Clue: It has a pink lake.

Bon Voyage!

Made in the USA
Middletown, DE
17 March 2022

62749444R00024

MW01070491

A Dog Named Munson and UGA® Traditions

©2018 Charlene Thomas.

Request for permission to make copies of any part of this work should be submitted online at info@mascotbooks.com or mailed to Mascot Books, 620 Herndon Parkway #320, Herndon, VA 20170.

If you would like a personalized copy of this book, please visit my web site at gameballseries.com.

The indicia featured in this book are protected trademarks of the University of Georgia.

PRT0322C

Third Edition, March 2022

Printed in the United States

ISBN: 978-1-64307-078-0

www.mascotbooks.com

Munson has learned a lot about UGA® and UGA® traditions. Munson wants to share these traditions with his friends.

A famous symbol on the UGA® campus is the Arch. The Arch is the official symbol of the University of Georgia®

The three columns of the arch represent wisdom, justice, and moderation.

It is a tradition that a student should not walk under the Arch until they graduate.

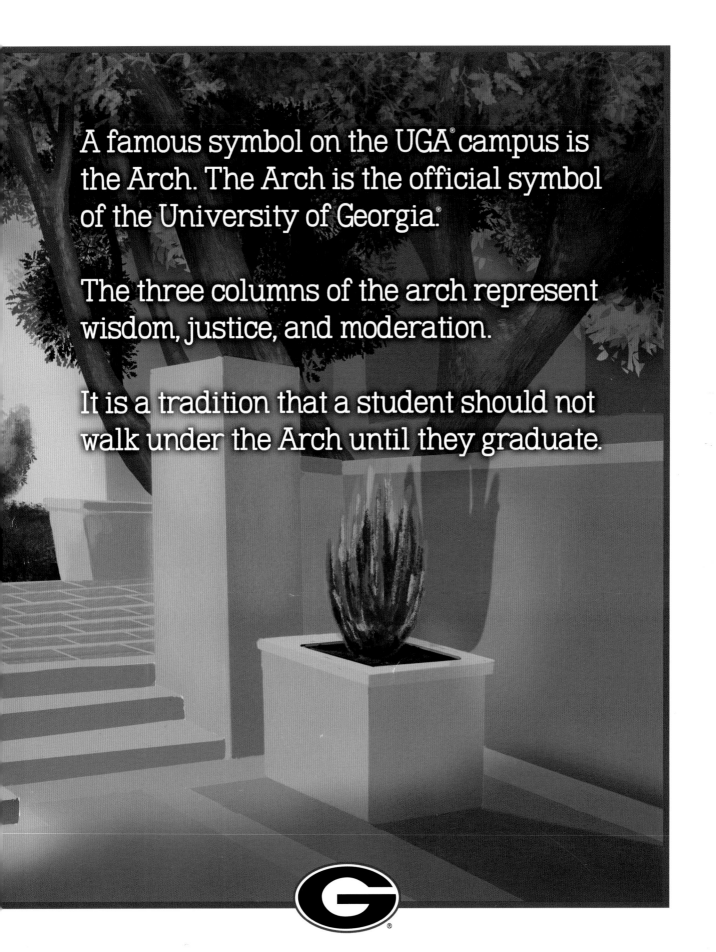

Students and fans ring the chapel bell after a Georgia® win.

CHAPEL BELL

Another Georgia® tradition is sitting with Ramsey. Bernard Ramsey was a dedicated UGA® grad who gave generously to his school.

The artwork of Jack Davis is a Georgia® tradition. His yearly drawings of UGA®'s mascot were eagerly awaited by Georgia® fans.

He always included names of his family on the arms of the Dawg.

He was a

Super Dawg.

Tailgating is a tradition on game day. Georgia® fans bring their tents and picnic food to enjoy while waiting for the game to start.

It's Saturda
in Athens

Munson loves for his friends to meet
Hairy Dawg. Hairy visits fans, cheers
on the Dawgs, and leads the Dawg Walk.

All Dawg fans love Uga, the UGA® mascot.
Uga is one of the best known mascots in the
country. Uga is a white English bulldog.
He rides to Athens in his red car.

He watches all the games from his doghouse located on the sideline of Sanford Stadium.

The Dawg Walk begins when the football players arrive at Sanford Stadium on team buses. The team and coaches walk to the stadium past the cheering fans and the Redcoat Band.

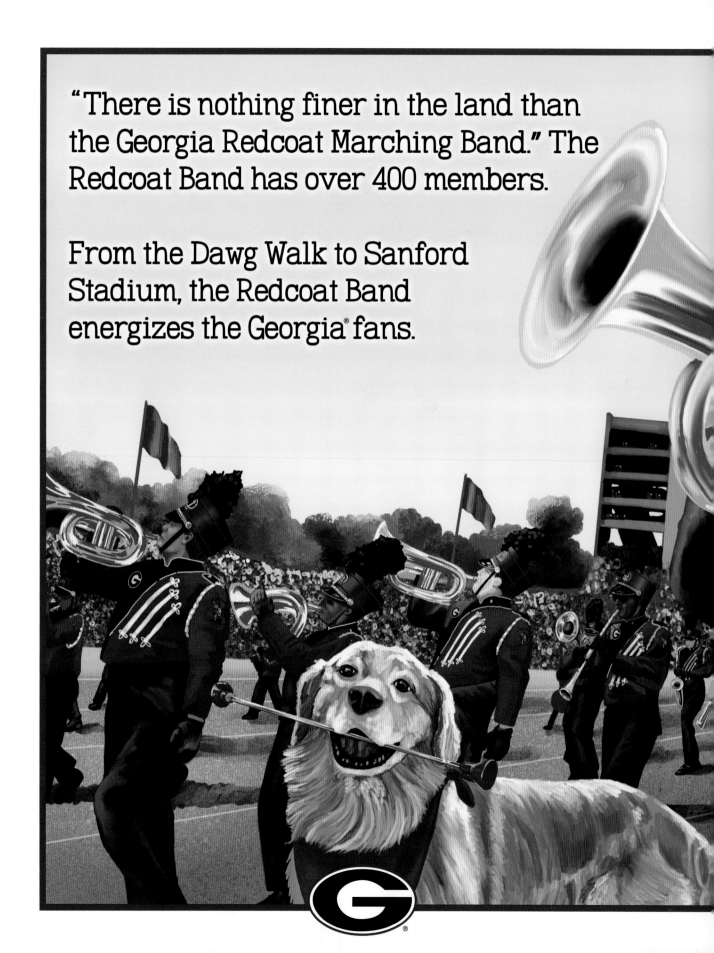

"There is nothing finer in the land than the Georgia Redcoat Marching Band." The Redcoat Band has over 400 members.

From the Dawg Walk to Sanford Stadium, the Redcoat Band energizes the Georgia® fans.

"The Lone Trumpeter" in the southwest corner of the upper deck plays the first fourteen notes of the "Bulldawg Battle Hymn" before each game starts.

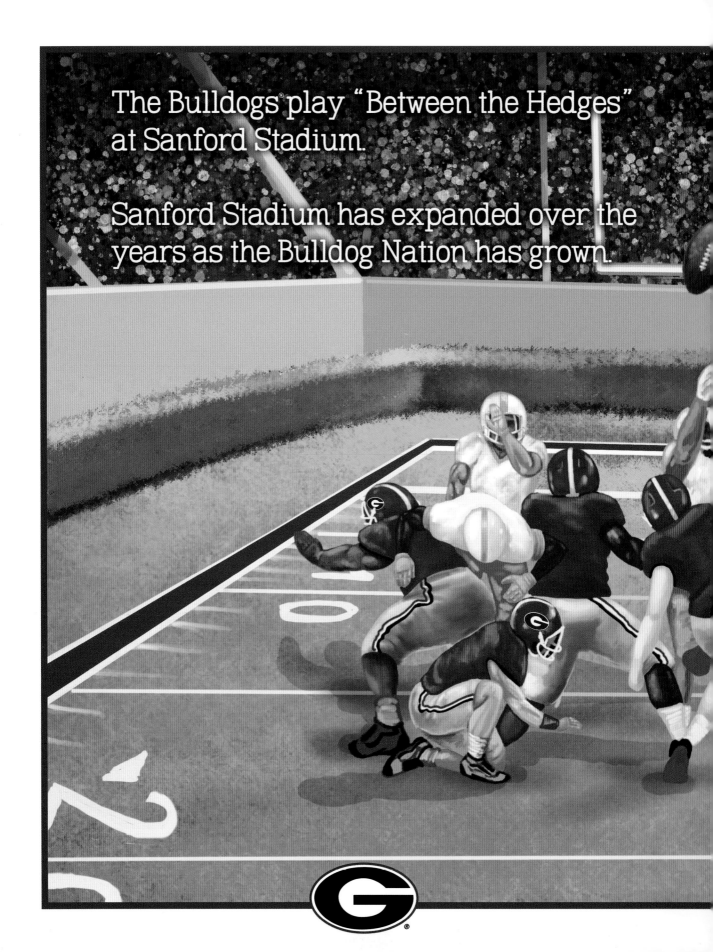

The Bulldogs® play "Between the Hedges" at Sanford Stadium.

Sanford Stadium has expanded over the years as the Bulldog Nation has grown.

The famous hedges have surrounded the playing field since the stadium was built.

The fans at Sanford Stadium call the Dawgs® before each kick off. Fans stand and yell...

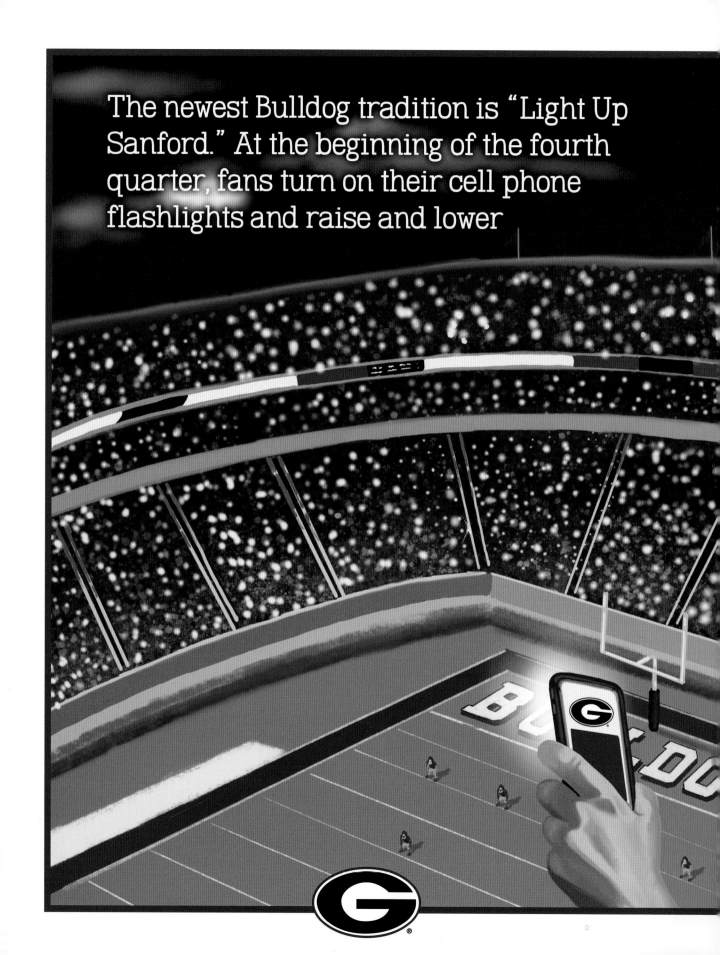

The newest Bulldog tradition is "Light Up Sanford." At the beginning of the fourth quarter, fans turn on their cell phone flashlights and raise and lower their arms as the Redcoat Band plays the "Krypton Fanfare." The lights show unity in the Bulldog Nation.

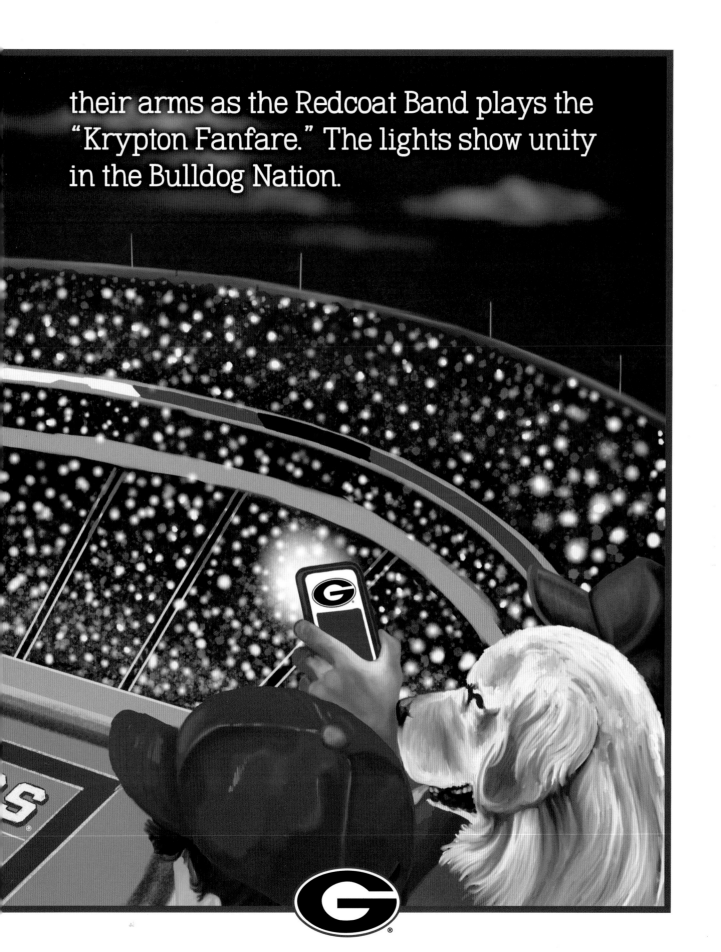

It is a tradition for Georgia® fans to sing the fight song "Glory Glory to Old Georgia®."

"Glory, glory to old Georgia!®
Glory, glory to old Georgia!®
Glory, glory to old Georgia!®
G-E-O-R-G-I-A!®"

Singing the song excites the crowd and helps young fans spell Georgia®

"Two words. Two simple words
which express the sentiments
of the entire Bulldog Nation...

Go Dawgs!®"

-Larry Munson
Famous UGA® Radio Announcer
1966-2008